For Jesse Edwards — in time for
the next adventure, welcome! ~ J L

LITTLE TIGER PRESS LTD,
an imprint of the Little Tiger Group
1 Coda Studios,
189 Munster Road,
London SW6 6AW
www.littletiger.co.uk

First published in Great Britain 2019
Text and illustrations copyright © Jonny Lambert 2019
Jonny Lambert has asserted his right to be identified as the author and
illustrator of this work under the Copyright, Designs and Patents Act, 1988
A CIP catalogue record for this book is available
from the British Library

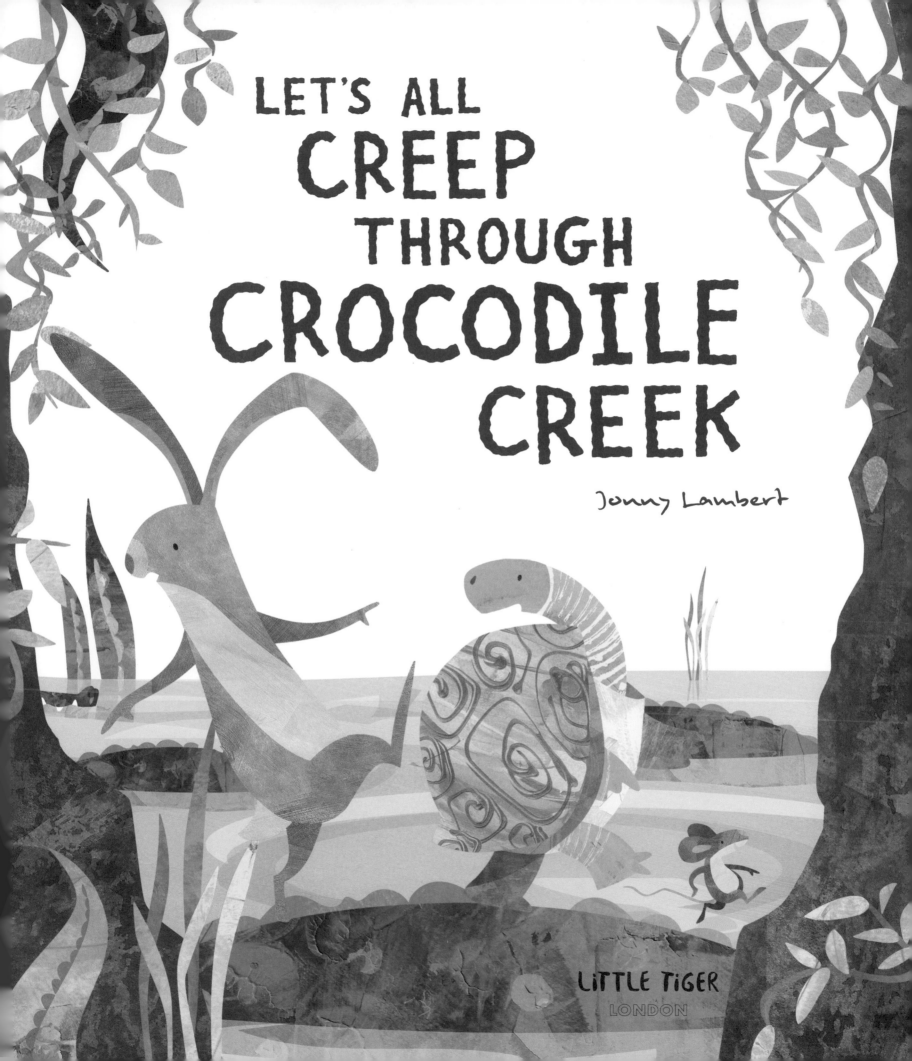

LET'S ALL CREEP THROUGH CROCODILE CREEK

Jonny Lambert

LITTLE TIGER

LONDON

The sun sank slowly in the sky.
  "We'd better get home before dark," said Mouse.
"Let's use the shortcut through the creek."

"Good question, Shelly," nodded Mouse,
as they all set off together.

A crocodile has a knobbly,
gnarly back.

Don't worry, Shelly.
You won't EVER meet a
crocodile in the creepy,
crooked creek!

On they went, swinging through dark green vines. "I almost forgot," chuckled Mouse. "Crocs also have flippy, whippy tails!"

Just like swingy, springy vines?

!!!

Yes! You're getting
the hang of this!

"Eek!" squeaked Shelly as they splish-splashed into a gloomy tunnel.

I'm guessing crocodiles have scary, starey eyes?

Yes, yes . . . great, googly ones to see in the dark! Come on, we're nearly home!

And away they all ran from the
sneaky, snappy crocodiles.

The moon glowed brightly in the sky.
"Now how do we get home?"
huffed Shelly.

Easy peasy,
we'll take a shortcut
through the forest . . .

The fearsome,
frightful forest?
Won't there be tigers?